A Billie B. MYSTERY

Code Breakers

By Sally Rippin

Illustrated by Aki Fukuoka

Kane Miller
A DIVISION OF EDC PUBLISHING

First American Edition 2014
Kane Miller, A Division of EDC Publishing

Text copyright © 2013 Sally Rippin
Illustrations copyright © 2013 Aki Fukuoka
Series design copyright © 2013 Hardie Grant Egmont

First published in Australia by Hardie Grant Egmont

For information contact:
Kane Miller, A Division of EDC Publishing
P.O. Box 470663
Tulsa, OK 74147-0663
www.kanemiller.com
www.edcpub.com
www.usbornebooksandmore.com

Library of Congress Control Number: 2013953409

Printed and bound in the United States of America
4 5 6 7 8 9 10
ISBN: 978-1-61067-312-9

Chapter One

Billie B. Brown sits on the front step of her house staring down at the sheet of paper on her lap. Next to her sits her best friend, Jack, jiggling his knees up and down with excitement.

The two friends can't tear themselves away from what they've just found. It's a note for the Secret Mystery Club. And it's in code!

"Can you believe it?" Billie whispers. "Someone knows about our Secret Mystery Club. And they've sent us a letter! I wish I could work out what it says."

"I wonder who wrote it?" says Jack.

Suddenly the front door opens. Billie quickly stuffs the paper into her pocket.

"There you are, Billie!" says her mom from the doorway. "I've been looking for you everywhere. Come on! It's nearly time to go on our picnic. And Jack, your mom's looking for you, too."

Jack jumps up. "See you, Billie," he says and trots down her front steps.

But just before he steps out of the gate and onto the sidewalk, he stops and calls out a little sound like this: "Cock-a-doodle-dooooo!"

4

Billie's mom looks at him strangely, but Billie giggles. It is their special call for the Secret Mystery Club.

"Cock-a-doodle-dooooo!" Billie calls back. "I'll bring the you-know-what to school tomorrow," she promises, patting her pocket.

"The what?" Billie's mom asks.

"Nothing!" Billie and Jack say together, grinning **mischievously**.

Then Jack jogs to the next gate along and runs up to his front door.

Billie steps inside her house. Her dad is on the phone in the family room. When he sees Billie he quickly says good-bye and hangs up.

"Who was that?" Billie asks.

"Oh, just Mika's mom," her dad says. "We were talking about something we're organizing for the school."

Billie shrugs and runs into the kitchen to find her little brother.

Noah is sitting on his booster seat at the table, snacking on some carrot sticks.

Billie runs up to him and gives him a big smoochy kiss right on his fat baby cheek. His hair is soft and he smells like strawberries.

"Oi!" he says crossly, pushing Billie away. "I eating!"

Billie giggles then spins around on the spot. "Cock-a-doodle-dooo!" she crows happily. Inside her chest she is **bubbling** with excitement. Inside her pocket is a real Secret Mystery to solve!

Chapter Two

The next day at school the Secret Mystery Club meet at recess under the big pepper tree in the playground.

Billie told Alex and Mika before school that she had something very exciting to show them.

"What is it?" Mika asks, sitting close so she can see what Billie has brought.

Billie smiles as she pulls the crumpled slip of paper out of her schoolbag. She opens it up and smooths it out so the others can see. "It's a secret note," Billie says.

"Wow," says Alex, peering down at the dark squiggly lines. "Where did you find it?"

"On my front step," Billie says.

"It was addressed to the Secret Mystery Club," Jack adds. "And it's written in code!"

"No, it's not," says Mika, turning the page the other way around. "It's in Japanese!"

"What?" says Billie. She's not sure if she feels **happy** or **annoyed** that Mika has cracked the code so easily. "Are you sure?"

Mika rolls her eyes. "Of course I'm sure. I can read Japanese, you know."

11

"What does it say, then?" Alex says.

Mika takes the paper from Billie and peers down at the scribbly characters. "It's a haiku," she says.

あかいみに
ひのでがさして
ひんとあり

"What's that?" Jack asks.

"I know!" Alex says. "It's a Japanese poem. It has three lines and it doesn't rhyme. That's right, isn't it, Mika?"

Mika nods. Then she reads aloud slowly, translating the Japanese into English.

"Children look for clues
In the red fruiting berries
When the sun is new."

She looks up at the others.

"What's that supposed to mean?" Billie frowns. "Why would someone send us a poem that makes no sense?" She feels a little disappointed.

13

"Don't you see?" Jack says. "We're the children. And we're looking for clues. It's about us!"

"So we have to look for clues in red fruiting berries…" Alex adds.

"Strawberries!" Mika says. "I have strawberries at my house. My mom is growing them."

"It could be apples. We have an apple tree," Billie suggests.

"Nah, it says berries, Billie," says Alex. "The next clue must be at Mika's house!"

"Let's go this afternoon!" Jack says **excitedly**.

"Wait," says Alex. "It says when the sun is new."

"Well, when's that?" Jack says.

"I don't know," Alex says.

"This poem doesn't make any sense!" Billie huffs.

"I think it means the morning," Mika says. "It's a Japanese expression."

"Oh!" says Alex, laughing.

"Of course! So there will be a clue for us in Mika's strawberry patch tomorrow morning. I get it! Make sure you bring the clue in to school tomorrow then, won't you, Mika?"

"Of course!" says Mika, grinning.

Just then the bell rings and they all stand up to go to class. Billie holds out her hand for the note.

"I'd better hold on to it," Mika says importantly, "seeing as I'm the only one here who can read Japanese."

Billie shrugs and slips her hand into her pocket.

As she walks back to class she feels a **jumbled—up** mix of feelings bubbling away in her tummy. She is excited about the mysterious letter, but she also feels a little bit annoyed that she couldn't work it out herself.

What's the point of writing a note to the Secret Mystery Club if only one of us can read it? she thinks grumpily.

Chapter Three

That night at the dinner table, Billie is especially quiet. Usually she and Noah joke around so much it drives their parents crazy, but tonight nothing seems to make her laugh.

Even when her little brother sings a funny song and tips his bowl of peas over his head, Billie just stares down at her plate, pushing her fork around.

"What's the matter, Billie?" her dad asks as he cleans up the mess. "You seemed so happy this morning. Is something wrong?"

Billie shrugs and jabs at a pea with the end of her fork. "It's nothing," she says.

The truth is that she feels silly for being so **grumpy**. It's just that the Secret Mystery Club was her idea. And she wasn't even able to solve their first real mystery.

Noah slips down from the table and trots toward Billie. "Here, Bee bee!" he says softly, calling her by the nickname he has given her. He takes her hand and slips something into it.

Billie looks down at what Noah has given her. It is his favorite red car.

"Thanks, Noah," Billie says, finally smiling. She kisses him on his soft brown hair. Noah can be the most annoying little brother in the world, but he can also be the best.

"Come on!" she says, hoisting him into her arms. "Let's play cars."

"Cars! Cars!" Noah shouts happily.

"Come back in twenty minutes," Billie's dad says, smiling. "I just have to make a quick phone call to Alex's dad. He has a drill I need to borrow. Then I'll make dessert."

"Can I have bananas and ice cream with sprinkles?" Billie asks.

"You bet!" says Billie's dad.

"Thanks, Dad," Billie says. Bananas and ice cream with sprinkles will definitely cheer her up!

Chapter Four

The next morning Billie and Jack meet Alex under the pepper tree before school.

Billie sits nervously looking out for Mika, who is late, as usual, because her mom has to drop her on her way to work.

Mika says her mom takes a long time getting ready in the mornings, so she is always running late. Billie can't wait to see what Mika has found in her mother's strawberry patch.

Alex paces up and down. "There she is!" he calls out. He points to a figure in the distance running toward them. They all run to meet her.

"Did you find something?" Jack asks.

Mika nods **excitedly** and pulls another paper envelope out of her pocket. This time the envelope is longer and has a little see-through window, like a bill or a letter from a bank. In the window it says:

```
Attention: Secret
    Mystery Club.
C/- Mrs.Okinawa's
strawberry patch.
```

Billie is relieved to see that Mika hasn't opened it yet.

27

"Wait! Can I see it first?" she begs, as Mika slips her finger under the sealed flap.

Mika hands Billie the envelope. Billie takes her magnifying glass out of her pocket and **inspects** the envelope carefully.

"Hmmm, it doesn't seem to have any fingerprints on it," she says. "And it looks like the letter has been typed on a computer. So it must have come from someone with a computer."

"Everybody has a computer, Billie!"
Alex snorts. "Come on, give it back
to Mika so she can open it."

Billie frowns at Alex and hands
the envelope back **reluctantly**.
She wishes the envelope had been
hidden in *her* garden!

Mika carefully opens the envelope
and slips the paper out. It is folded
into three. When she smooths it
out and they see what is typed
there, they all gasp in surprise.

"Well, that's not Japanese!" Jack jokes, looking down at the page.

Mika giggles. "That's for sure!"

Billie frowns. There are random numbers typed in lines across the page.

"What could all those numbers mean? How can we possibly understand that?" Billie says, feeling confused.

"Give it to Alex," Jack suggests. "He's good at math."

Alex peers down at the note. This is what is written on it:

20-15   6-9-14-4   20-8-5

14-5-24-20   14-15-20-5

12-15-15-11   21-14-4-5-18

20-8-5 18-5-4

20-18-1-9-14   19-5-20

"Do you think they're math problems?" Jack asks Alex.

Alex shrugs. "Maybe. Leave it with me," he says importantly, as the bell rings. "I'll try and work it out today."

32

Before Billie can even say anything, Alex and Mika start heading to class. Billie trudges behind them with Jack, her head hung low.

I should be happy that we are getting all these secret mystery notes, she thinks. *But now that's two codes I couldn't crack. I'm a terrible detective!*

"What's the matter?" Jack asks. He is smiling kindly.

Billie wants to tell him how she feels, but she is worried he might think she is silly.

33

So instead of telling Jack, she just says, "Nothing," and tries to smile. But her smile comes out **crooked** and **wobbly** and Jack looks at her like he doesn't quite believe her.

In class Billie finds it hard to concentrate. She keeps thinking about that mysterious note with its tricky-looking code.

She can't even talk about it with her friends because Mr. Benetto has already separated them for talking too much.

Billie thinks that if she could crack the code before Alex she would feel like she was an important member of the Secret Mystery Club again. She wishes she had it in front of her so she could try and work it out.

"Billie! Are you paying attention?" Mr. Benetto says.

Oh no! Billie looks up quickly.

Mr. Benetto's voice sounds cross, but his eyes are smiling. "What's the answer to question seven?" he asks.

Billie looks down at her work sheet. "Um, I'm not sure," she replies, feeling **embarrassed**.

"You need to listen more carefully, Billie," says Mr. Benetto.

Lola sticks up her hand. "The answer is seventy-six, Mr. Benetto!"

"Thank you, Lola," Mr. Benetto says. "Perhaps you can sit next to Billie for the rest of the lesson to help her with the work sheet?"

Oh no, that's all I need! Billie sighs.

Sometimes Lola is OK, but sometimes she can be very bossy.

Just then Billie has an idea.
A super-duper idea!

"Hey, Lola," Billie whispers, when Lola sits down next to her, "do you know anything about codes?"

"Why?" Lola says suspiciously.

"No reason," Billie says quickly.
"Just wondering."

"Actually I have a book about codes," Lola says. "What kind of code?"

"A code in numbers," Billie says.

"Oh, that's easy!" Lola says. "Each number is probably a letter of the alphabet. 1 equals A, 2 equals B, and so on."

"That's it!" Billie squeals.

"Girls — is that math you're doing?" Mr. Benetto says.

"Um, kind of." Billie giggles, jiggling in her seat. She can't wait until recess to tell the others.

Chapter Five

As soon as the bell rings, Billie runs out to the playground with her friends.

"I've got it! I've got it!" she yells as soon as they have reached the pepper tree. "I've cracked the code!"

"So have I!" Alex says. "And I've already worked out the message. I did it in class. See?" He unfolds the paper. There, underneath the rows of numbers, is his neat handwriting:

20-15 6-9-14-4 20-8-5
TO FIND THE

14-5-24-20 14-15-20-5
NEXT NOTE

12-15-15-11 21-14-4-5-18
LOOK UNDER

20-8-5 18-5-4
THE RED

20-18-1-9-14 19-5-20
TRAIN SET

Billie's heart sinks like a stone. "How did you work it out?"

Alex shrugs. "It was easy. It's an alphabet code. 1 is A, 2 is B and so on. It didn't take me long. And I've already worked out what the red train set is. It's an old train set of my dad's in our toy cupboard. That's where the next clue will be."

"Good work!" says Jack, patting Alex on the back.

"Yeah, it was pretty clever to work that out, Alex," Mika says. "Wasn't it, Billie?"

"Uh-huh," Billie says quietly. She knows she should be **happy** that they have worked out the code, but she can't help it. *She* was going to crack that code.

Billie feels like she might cry. While the others are looking at the note again, she walks quickly away.

43

Billie goes to the monkey bars
and climbs up to the very top.
There, she can let the big salty
tears stream down her face without
anyone seeing them.

Before very long, a head pokes over
the top of the monkey bars. It is
Jack, making a funny face.

Billie wipes her eyes on her sleeve.
Even though she is feeling **mad**
and **sad** and all kinds of horrible
feelings bunched up together, she
still can't help smiling when she
sees Jack's silly expression.

He climbs up and sits beside her. "What's up?" he says.

Billie scrunches up her face and sniffs. "It's stupid," she says, embarrassed. "You probably won't even want to be my friend anymore if I tell you."

"Billie!" says Jack, rolling his eyes. "Haven't we been friends forever?"

Billie nods.

"Haven't we told each other all of our secrets?"

Billie nods again.

"Well?" Jack says, raising his eyebrows and waiting.

Billie takes a deep breath. She looks down at the playground and sees Mika and Alex sitting together under the pepper tree.

"I feel left out," she says in a little voice. "All of you have been able to work out the codes except me. Now I don't feel like I should be a member of the Secret Mystery Club any more because I'm such a bad detective.

47

Alex and Mika probably don't even want me in the club now."

Billie knows this last bit isn't really true. Alex and Mika are her friends too. But she really wants Jack to understand how upset she is feeling so she decides there is no harm in exaggerating just a **teensy** bit.

"What are you talking about?" Jack says. "I haven't cracked a code yet either. Only Mika and Alex have. And they were just lucky. Of course we want you in the club!

There wouldn't even be a Secret Mystery Club without you!"

"I guess so," Billie sniffs. It is true that Jack hasn't cracked a code yet either. She had forgotten that.

Jack thinks for a minute. "How about we ask Mika and Alex if when we get the next code, you can have first try at cracking it? That would be fair."

Billie smiles a little smile. "Thanks, Jack," she says. "You're a good friend. I know I'm just being silly."

Jack grins. "If you don't stop being grumpy, I'll be your only friend!" he jokes.

Billie giggles. She swings her legs happily in the empty space beneath them, her heart feeling **warm** again. "Who do you think is sending us all these weird notes, anyway?"

"No idea," Jack says, swinging his legs alongside her. "It's fun though, isn't it?"

"Sure is," Billie says. She can't wait to crack tomorrow's code.

Chapter Six

For the rest of the day, Billie listens carefully in class. She doesn't want to get in trouble with Mr. Benetto again. Billie likes Mr. Benetto and she hates getting in trouble.

Billie is very excited that she will soon have a code to crack.

Even sitting next to bossy Lola doesn't feel so bad now. And when Mr. Benetto springs a surprise quiz about marsupials on the class, Billie and Lola win the competition!

When school is over Billie meets Jack at the bike shed like she always does. Jack pulls out his scooter from the tangled mess of bikes and Billie hops on her bike.

"What do you think the next code is going to be?" Billie asks excitedly as they ride home together.

"I don't know," Jack says, scooting along beside her.

"Alex had better not open the envelope before he gets to school," Billie says.

"He won't," says Jack. "He promised."

That night, Billie has a nightmare. She is trapped in a room with a witch who has long white hair and long yellow fingernails.

The witch is dipping her fingernail into a bucket of red paint and using it to write big **squiggly** letters on a white wall. Billie knows that if she can't work out what the code means she will never find her way out of the witch's room.

She wakes up shivering and shaking. "Mom?" she calls out softly. "Dad?"

After a moment, Billie sees the light in the hall switch on and her dad pokes his head around the door.

"Are you OK?" he whispers. "Mom's asleep."

"Can you give me a cuddle?" Billie says in a little voice. She knows she sounds like a baby, but she can't help it. "I had a nightmare."

"Of course," Billie's dad says. He crosses the room in three long strides and plonks down on the bed next to Billie.

She sits up and he gives her a big warm hug as tight as a bear's.

Billie feels her body stop shivering.

"What was your nightmare about?" Billie's dad asks.

"Witches," Billie says. "And codes."

"Codes?" he asks.

"Yes. Like codes a detective would crack. A good detective, that is," she sighs.

"Well, I'm sure every detective has different skills," her dad says. "Some might be good with language codes and others with number codes."

Billie looks up at her dad in surprise. Does he know something?

No, it's impossible! All her friends promised to keep the club a secret.

She decides to test him all the same. "What kind of code would you use to write a coded note?" she asks, watching him carefully.

"Oh, me?" says her dad. "I don't know anything about codes. You know me, I prefer baking cookies. Especially lemon cookies," he says mysteriously.

"What's that supposed to mean?" Billie says, giggling.

"Oh, nothing," says her dad. "I just thought I might make some lemon cookies this week. I like to use my secret recipe."

"Secret recipe?" Billie asked, feeling curious. "What do you mean?"

"Well, I have to hide it so no one can steal my secret," he explains. "It's hidden in a place only I know how to find. A warm place. A very warm place, in fact."

Billie thinks her dad is acting very strangely. *Is he trying to tell me something?* she wonders.

But before she can ask, he kisses her on her forehead and tucks her blanket in.

"All right, time for sleep now," he says. "School tomorrow."

Billie snuggles into bed and thinks happily about tomorrow's code.

She hopes it will be easy for her to crack it. But it would also be nice if it was a little bit hard, so that her friends will know what a good detective she is!

Chapter Seven

Alex is already waiting under the pepper tree when Billie and Jack arrive at school the next day.

"It's here!" Alex calls, waving a brown paper envelope in the air. "It's here!"

Billie and Jack run up to him.

61

"Pass it to me?" Billie begs excitedly. "Remember you said I could look at it first!"

Alex shakes his head. "We have to wait for Mika. That's the rule."

"All right," Billie nods, but her fingers twitch in frustration. *Hurry up, Mika!* she thinks impatiently, but she knows it's not Mika's fault she is always late.

Finally Mika arrives, just as the bell goes. Billie, Jack and Alex run up to her at the school gate.

"Quick! Quick!" Billie says. "Let me open the letter!"

Alex hands the envelope to Billie who rips it open, almost tearing the paper inside. She pulls it out and the four of them stare at what is written there.

,llaw eht no ,rorrim ,rorriM
?lla ta eton siht daer uoy nac

.yaw eht dael neht ,nac uoy fI
.yawa raf ton s'eton tsal ruoY

.tsaeb a htiw sevil uoy fo enO

tsael ron tsal rehtien era uoY

.dehs a rednu ,kcatsyah a rednU

.deb ruoy rednu em dnif lliw uoY

"It's backward!" blurts Jack.
Then suddenly he turns very red.
"Oh gosh, Billie!" he says, clamping
his hand over his mouth, a horrified
look on his face.

Billie gasps. "You promised, Jack!"

"I didn't mean it!" he says.

"I'm sorry! I really am! It's just that Dad and I were doing backward spelling only last night. That's how he teaches me how to spell hard words. I wasn't thinking. Please don't be mad at me!"

But Billie feels her heart grow as heavy as a stone. She knows Jack didn't mean to crack the code. But she still feels hurt and her head sizzles angrily. She shoves the note into Jack's hands. "You work it out then!" she says gruffly.

"I guess you're better off without me after all."

Then she storms off to class, tears springing into her eyes.

But as soon as Billie sits down at her desk she feels bad. Jack is her best friend. She knows he wouldn't say anything to upset her on purpose.

Then she thinks about the joke he made yesterday — that if she got any grumpier she would have no friends at all!

He's right, Billie thinks. *This is a Secret Mystery CLUB. It doesn't matter who cracks the codes. We're all in this together.*

Billie makes a **promise** to herself that she will be much nicer to her friends in the future. Even if things do seem a little bit unfair.

When the bell rings for recess, Billie takes her time going out to the playground. Her friends are all waiting for her under the pepper tree.

68

"I'm really sorry," Billie says to Jack, hanging her head. "I shouldn't have shouted at you. I just feel so bad that I haven't been able to crack any of the codes. You're all so much better at this than me."

"No, we're not!" Mika says. "Mine was just easy because it was in Japanese."

"And mine was easy for me because I'm good with numbers." Alex shrugs.

"And my dad always writes notes for me in backward writing," Jack says.

Billie frowns, thinking about what her friends have said. "It's a bit weird, isn't it?" she says. "It's like each note was meant for one of us."

"Very weird," agrees Mika. "They must have been written by someone who knows us well."

"Wait," says Jack. "If there is a note for each of us then that means…"

"There's one note left!" Billie realizes happily. "For me!"

Jack nods, smiling. "I wrote the note out in class," he says, pulling the rumpled paper out of his pocket.

They all gather around to read it.

Mirror, mirror, on the wall,
can you read this note at all?

If you can, then lead the way.
Your last note's not far away.

One of you lives with a beast.
You are neither last nor least.

Under a haystack, under a shed.
You will find me under your bed.

Jack looks up at them all. "There's one last note," he explains. "And it's under my bed."

"How do you know it's your bed?" Mika asks.

Jack grins. "That's what my dad calls our dog. The Beast."

"Scraps isn't exactly a beast!" Alex says, laughing.

The others giggle.

"So, when we crack the last code, we'll be able to solve the mystery of where the notes are leading us," Jack says. "And I have a feeling the last clue will be for Billie."

Billie feels her heart soar. *The last clue is mine!* she thinks happily.

Chapter Eight

The Secret Mystery Club decide
they can't wait until the next day
to find the letter, so they all ask
their parents if they can go to Jack's
house after school.

As soon as they arrive, the four
of them run up to Jack's room.

Sure enough, in the dust and gloom under his bed, a little white envelope shines brightly.

Jack pulls it out and hands it to Billie. "The last letter!" he says.

The others all gather around Billie, waiting.

"Open it! Open it!" Mika begs.

Billie sits cross-legged on the floor with the envelope in her hands. Written across the front in pale blue writing, are the words:

To the Secret Mystery Club
TOP SECRET!

Her heart is flipping around like a bird. *What if I can't crack this code?* she worries. Then she reminds herself: *Of course I'll be able to! This one's for ME!*

With trembling hands, Billie pulls open the seal and reaches inside the envelope for the slip of paper. Then she unfolds it and smooths it on the floor in front of her.

Everyone gasps.

There is nothing written there. Nothing at all.

"I can't believe it," Jack says quietly. He puts his hand on Billie's shoulder.

Billie stares down at the paper. She can't believe it either. How could the very last note — *her* note — have nothing written on it? Is this an awful trick? Is there nothing at the end of this trail of notes after all?

But then an idea comes to her.

Someone knew Mika could read Japanese, she thinks. And that Alex was good with numbers and Jack could read backward. She remembers her dad telling her that every detective has different skills.

Suddenly, Billie has the answer. She looks up at her friends. "Don't worry!" she says, grinning. "I think I know how to read the note. Follow me!" She stands up with the letter in her hand and dashes out of Jack's room.

Chapter Nine

Jack, Mika and Alex run after
Billie, down the stairs, through
the kitchen, out the back door
and into Jack's backyard. One by
one, they squeeze through
the hole in the fence and into
Billie's backyard.

80

Billie waits impatiently for them at the back door to her house. "Dad's baking!" she says. "And I'll bet they're lemon cookies."

The others look at each other, confused.

"Come on!" says Billie, leading them into the kitchen. The oven is on, but her dad has left the room. She can hear him talking to Noah upstairs.

Billie runs to the oven and flattens the paper onto the warm glass.

Nothing happens for a moment. Billie holds her breath, crossing her fingers. Then slowly, as they watch, pale brown letters and shapes begin to appear across the page.

Mika gasps. "How did you do that?"

"It's written in lemon juice," Billie explains. "Dad and I saw it on a science show once. When the lemon juice heats up, the writing turns brown."

As they stare at the paper five letters and a drawing appears:

"What does that mean?" Alex says.

"Well, that's an apple tree, obviously," Billie says. "SMC is us. And HQ stands for headquarters."

"Secret Mystery Club Headquarters apple tree?" Jack says, frowning.

Billie dashes out the back door again. "Follow me!" she yells over her shoulder.

She runs all the way to the end of her backyard, with the others close behind.

There, by the chicken coop, is their enormous apple tree. Dangling from its branches is a long, thin cord.

Billie pulls it, and a rope ladder comes tumbling down. She squeals in delight.

Billie scrambles up the ladder and gasps when she sees what is hidden there.

"It's a tree house!" she yells to the others down below. "Oh, wow, it's wonderful! Come up – it's the coolest thing you've ever seen."

One by one, the others climb up the ladder to the platform of the little wooden tree house.

Billie feels like her heart might **burst** with happiness.

85

It's the most perfect tree house she could ever imagine, just big enough for four people, and hidden away from the world. "This can be our clubhouse!" Billie says. "The SMC headquarters. Just like it said on the note."

"This is incredible!" Jack says.

"It's beautiful!" Mika sighs.

"Amazing!" says Alex. "Who could have built it?"

Billie peers out through the leaves across her backyard.

From where she is sitting she has a perfect view of their kitchen. Through the windows she can see her dad inside, taking the lemon cookies out of the oven.

At that moment he looks up and gives a little wave. Billie smiles. "I think I know," she says.

Jack looks down and sees Billie's dad too. "Your dad?"

Billie nods. "He's been acting very weird lately. And he borrowed tools from Alex's dad the other day."

"But how could he have done it without you noticing?" Jack asks.

"Well, I've been kind of busy," Billie says. "Following a trail of secret notes. And cracking codes!"

"What? You think he wrote all those notes, too?" Mika says. "But he can't write Japanese!"

"No, but your mom can," Billie says. "And Jack's dad is very good at backward writing."

"Oh!" says Alex. "You think all our parents were in on it?"

Billie shrugs. "Dad was on the phone to your parents a lot this week."

It is all coming together now in Billie's mind.

"But, hold on," Alex says, frowning. "How did your dad even know about our club? I thought we had all sworn not to tell anyone!"

Billie looks at Jack. His cheeks turn very pink.

"That was my fault," he says quietly.

"I got scared when Billie was talking about the Spooky House.

90

I told my mom about it. She must have told Billie's dad."

"It's not your fault," Billie says. "It was my fault for scaring you. And besides, if my dad hadn't found out about the club he might never have built us this amazing clubhouse!"

"Or organized all those codes to crack!" Mika agrees.

"Yeah, I guess it doesn't matter," Alex says. "As long as it's only our parents. But no one else, OK?"

"OK!" everyone agrees. Then Jack does the SMC rooster call just to seal the deal and everyone laughs.

"It doesn't feel like we solved a real mystery though," Mika sighs. "Now that we know our parents set it up."

"Yeah, I wish we had a *real* mystery to solve," Alex agrees.

They all look at Billie.

Billie is thinking about something. She picks a leaf from the apple tree and rolls it between her fingers.

92

Finally she turns to them.

"I think I have the perfect mystery," she says, smiling. "Meet me in the playground before school tomorrow."

"What is it?" says Alex eagerly.

"You'll have to wait and see," says Billie. "But don't worry. You won't be disappointed."

To be continued...